How to Put Your Parents to Bed

By Mylisa Larsen

Illustrated by Babette Cole

KATHERINE TEGEN BOOKS
An Imprint of HarperCollins Publishers

Katherine Tegen Books is an imprint of HarperCollins Publishers.

How to Put Your Parents to Bed
Text copyright © 2016 by Mylisa Larsen. Illustrations copyright © 2016 by Babette Cole

ISBN 978-0-06-232064-3

The artist used midnight oil and mashed brain acrylic to create the illustrations for this book with a little help from dip
pen and ink, Dr. Ph. Martin's concentrated watercolor dye, watercolor crayons, and Rembrandt pastel.
Typography by Dana Fritts
15 16 17 18 19 SCP 10 9 8 7 6 5 4 3 2 1
❖
First Edition

To the unruly Larsen clan.
For goodness' sake, go to bed.

—M.L.

For Cecily and Beatrice.

—B.C.

I know.
You are not tired.

You could scale a tall tower.

You could sail savage seas.

You could paint a masterpiece.

It's bedtime, but bed is the last place
you want to be.

Adventures are out there waiting.
But have you looked at your parents?

Poor things.
Just between you and me,
they are not looking their best.

They need to go

to BED.

Parents are not good at going to bed.

"I have to put in a load of laundry," they say.

"I need to do the dishes."

"Just one more email."

It's one excuse after another with them.
You need to take charge.
Take the plate out of their hands.
Gently close the computer.
Tell them, "It's time for bed."

Start with brushing teeth.
They will argue.
They will say they'll do it later.

Squeeze out the toothpaste and get them brushing.

Help them if you can.
Those back molars can be
hard to reach.

Next get them into their pajamas.
You will be amazed how long this takes.

Parents get distracted by the smallest things.

Phones. Magazines. TV.

The cat.

Be patient.
Keep them moving toward the bedroom.

If you let them sit down,
they will fall asleep anywhere.

Sleeping parents are extremely hard to move.

Some of them SNORE.

Now, some parents become unruly
when faced with actually getting in bed.
Tiny things upset them.

They can

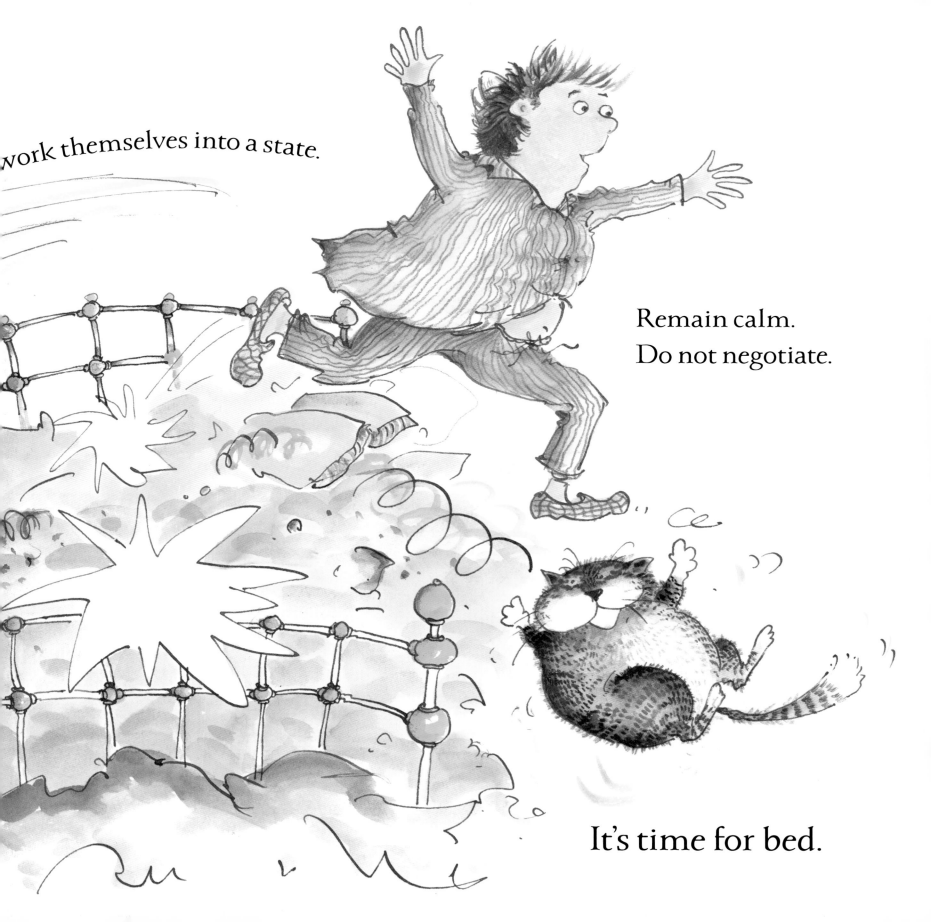

work themselves into a state.

Remain calm.
Do not negotiate.

It's time for bed.

This next part is tricky.
Stories.

Parents love stories at bedtime,

but they can get set in their ways.
They may insist on only hearing their favorites.

If they are used to three stories,
they want three stories.

Not two. Not one. No surprises.

You would think at this point
that you are almost there.
Your parents are in bed, teeth brushed,
pajamas on, stories read.

But this is when something unexpected always comes up.

Their favorite pillow is missing.

They want to check on the dog.

Their socks itch.

Tell yourself that this is almost over.

Handle

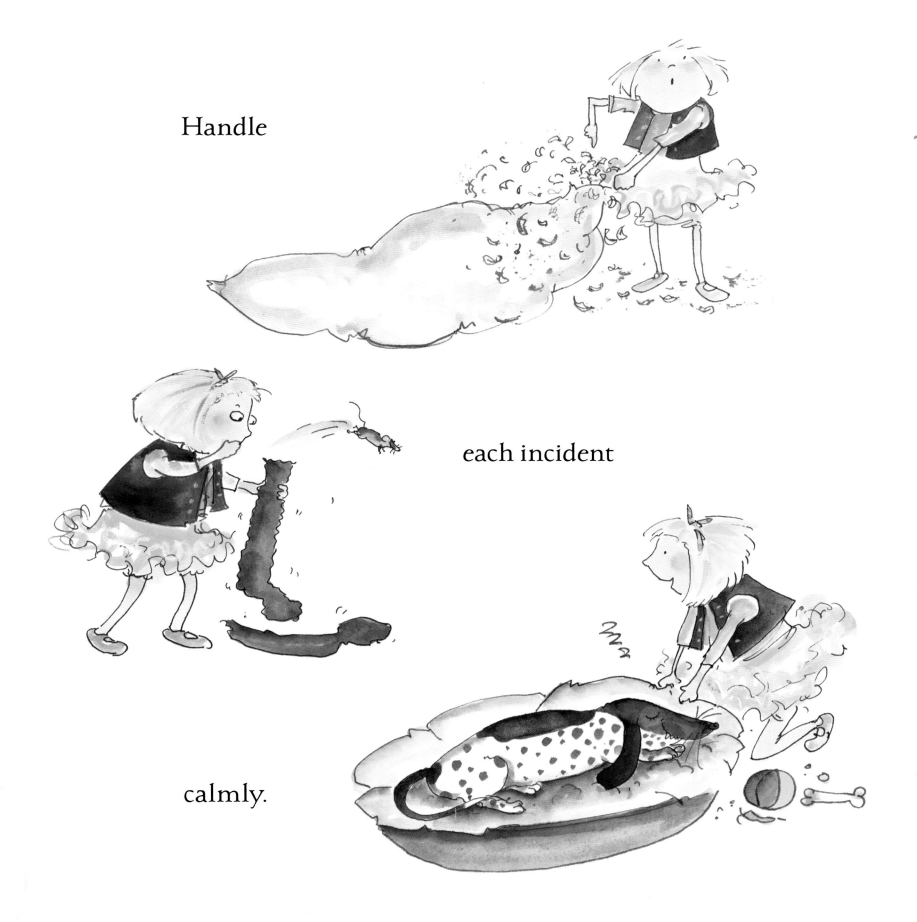

each incident

calmly.

Tuck them in.

Kiss them good-night.

Remind your parents that
they are NOT
to make phone calls
when you leave the room.

Better yet, take their cell phones.

Close the door.
Listen to make sure they're quiet.

Take a bow.
You have gotten your parents off to bed.
Now you can finally enjoy
some time for yourself.

But just between you and me,
you are not looking your best.

You look exhausted.

Maybe you need to go to bed.